the lost diary of Sami Star

**ALSO BY KAREN McCOMBIE
FOR BARRINGTON STOKE:**

The Girl with the Sunshine Smile

Candy Girl

Running from the Rainbow

Sweetness and Lies

Honey and Me

The OMG Blog

The Mystery of Me

the lost diary of Sami Star

KAREN McCOMBIE

WITH ILLUSTRATIONS BY
KATIE KEAR

Barrington Stoke

For Little Miss Sunshine, Carrie Joyce

1046783

First published in 2018 in Great Britain by
Barrington Stoke Ltd
18 Walker Street, Edinburgh, EH3 7LP

www.barringtonstoke.co.uk

Text © 2018 Karen McCombie
Illustrations © 2018 Katie Kear

The moral right of Karen McCombie and Katie Kear to be
identified as the author and illustrator of this work has been
asserted in accordance with the Copyright, Designs and
Patents Act, 1988

A CIP catalogue record for this book is available
from the British Library upon request

ISBN: 978-1-78112-816-9

Printed in China by Leo

CONTENTS

CHAPTER 1
HELLO? AM I INVISIBLE?

"Leave me *alone*!"

"Victoria! Listen to your mother!"

Uh-oh. My stupid family are at it *again*.

That's my dad I can hear, shouting at my big sister. Dad only calls her Victoria when he's angry. The rest of the time he calls her Vix, like everyone else does.

Every single day, my big sister and my parents argue about something.

Mum nags Vix about all the dirty mugs stashed in her room. Vix snaps at Mum for making a fuss over nothing. Dad narks about Vix playing her music too loud. Vix growls about Mum and Dad treating her like a kid.

What is it today? I think to myself.

"No – I won't. I'm *sick* of this, Mum!" Vix shouts.

"Don't talk to your mother like that, Victoria! Come back and say sorry this minute or—"

Slam!!!

Vix has stormed out of the living room and whacked the door shut.

I stand frozen half-way up the stairs. The thing is, I don't want to get in the middle of this war zone – I've tried before, but nobody takes any notice. Sometimes I feel like saying

"Hello? I'm Hannah. Can you see me? Or am I invisible?"

But now Vix spots me.

"They won't let it go, Hannah!" she says as she grabs her jacket from the coat rack. "How many times have I said I don't want to go to university?"

"Lots," I murmur.

She's said it non-stop over the last months. And now that A levels are coming up, Mum and Dad are going on at Vix even more.

"And what did Mum just do?" says Vix as she throws on her coat. "She showed me a newspaper article saying it's not too late to apply!"

At least they're arguing about the actual problem. I'm fed up with all the smaller fights about silly stuff like messy mugs. The real problem is that Mum and Dad think that:

* Vix is a total brainiac, and

* she's gone totally mad.

"I mean, don't they understand that *not everyone wants to go to university?*" shouts Vix.

She's not shouting because I'm deaf. She's shouting so Mum and Dad can hear loud and clear through the living-room door.

Slam!!!

I'm sure Mum and Dad heard that too – it's the front door this time, and Vix is gone.

There's a stunned silence, then I hear Mum and Dad ask each other what they're going to do about Vix. They're always saying the same thing in the same frantic way. They've asked each other this a million times before, and I'm fed up with it.

Fed up that Vix and Mum and Dad never listen to each other. Fed up that no one listens to *me*.

Do any of them know that I got the lead part in the school play? Or that my favourite teacher, Ms Barr, is leaving to have a baby? Do any of them know I'm finding Maths really hard at the moment? Or that I've had this on-and-off pain in my tummy for ages, which I'm pretty sure is down to stress? My good stuff, my bad stuff – none of it is important.

In the last few weeks, it's like the colour has drained out of our happy home. Life in the house feels black and white – and it feels like there's a blinding spotlight pointing straight at Vix. No one even sees me. I'm in the shadows.

Well, I need them to see me too.

I shrug on my jacket, grab my bag and slip out of the door with only a soft click of the lock.

I don't think my parents will even spot that I've gone ...

CHAPTER 2
THE LOST DIARY

I escape to the park and message my best friends Robyn and Zadie. When I get there, they're waiting for me on a bench in the late-afternoon sunshine.

"Is it bad again at home, Hannah?" asks Zadie, and she tips her head to one side.

"Same pointless argument, same pointless shouting," I say with a sigh.

I begin to moan about how awful things are between my parents and Vix – till I see that

Robyn isn't listening. She's looking down at her phone, swipe, swipe, swiping madly at the screen.

Is she maybe looking for a picture of a cute kitten or one of those funny sarky quotes to cheer me up?

"OMG, check out Jade's jeans. How bad are they?" says Robyn, and holds up her phone.

Oh … so Robyn wasn't trying to find a cute baby animal or something to make me smile. She was just zipping through her Instagram feed cos I was boring her with my problems.

"Where do you even *get* jeans as bad as that?" Zadie joins in. "Are they from the market or something?"

"See? Aren't they the *worst*, Hannah?" says Robyn. She swivels her phone around.

I look at the photo of Jade and her baggy jeans.

I don't really care about Jade's jeans and if they're bad or not. But I do care that my best friends are being pretty mean. Cos maybe Jade *did* get her jeans from the market. So what? Maybe she loves them. Or maybe she's embarrassed about them but they're all her mum could afford.

When did Robyn and Zadie get like this? In primary school we used to have such a laugh. But since we went to secondary school it's all about how they look or picking over other people's style. And they never have anything nice to say about any—

"Whoah ... what *is* that?" Robyn suddenly snaps.

She twists round and looks over the back of the park bench.

Me and Zadie look too.

On the grass is a thick, square book, like a chunky photo album. I jump up, go round the bench and pick it up.

"Must have fallen out of someone's bag," I say as I brush away dirt and blades of grass from the sky-blue cover.

"Whatever – just hurry up and open it, Hannah," says Zadie as soon as I sit back down.

I'm already tugging at the blue ribbon that holds the book closed.

"*This diary belongs to Sami Star*," I read on the first page.

The handwriting is interesting, arty. The fine thin pen turns the bottom of the "y" and the "g" into gorgeous little swirls. Teeny stars are drawn all around the words.

"*Sami Star?* What kind of name is *that*?" snorts Robyn.

"Who cares?" says Zadie. She's all excited. "It's a diary! Could be some good gossip in here. Get on with it, Hannah!"

I get on with it. I turn page after page.

There is no gossip.

Every double page is the same but different. The day and date are hand-written at the top. There is a Polaroid photo looking down at a pair of feet and another of a hairstyle. Different shoes, socks or tights and different hairstyles.

Each entry has a section with the title *Best thing about today* in that lovely, swirly handwriting.

"*Best thing about today – snuggling with Buster, the darlingest dog in the world,*" Zadie reads aloud with a sneer on her face. "How lame *is* that?"

It doesn't seem that lame to me. There's a really good doodly drawing of a pug right by the entry. I wish I could draw that well. Or have a pug that cute.

"This is one *dumb* diary," says Robyn as she turns a few more pages.

"Actually, with all the photos and notes, it's more like a scrapbook," I reply.

"Yeah, a book that needs to be scrapped!" giggles Zadie.

She grabs Sami Star's diary from me – and with a quick flick of her hand she throws it in the nearby bin. It lands with a dull *clonk*.

"Come on, let's go to the cafe," says Robyn, yawning. Zadie gets up and sets off along the path beside her.

I'm about to follow my friends too, then I stop and do something before they notice.

I rescue the lost diary of Sami Star from the bin and stuff it in my bag ...

Best thing about today...

Snuggling with Buster,
the darlingest dog in
the world!

CHAPTER 3

SORRY FOR SOMEONE I'VE NEVER MET

Yesterday evening I stayed in my room, well away from my family and all their battles.

I wasn't lonely – Sami Star kept me company. Or at least her diary did. I looked over it for hours, checking out her sweetly odd style, her interesting snaps, beautiful doodles and short bursts of writing.

And today I'm home from school and back in my room again, day-dreaming through Sami's diary one more time. I'm concentrating on the photos at the moment – her dog Buster as he jumps up on his back legs or gets his tummy tickled by a hand that *has* to belong to Sami. A photo of a hugging, happy blonde lady and a smiling Asian-looking man (*Mummy and Daddy*, Sami has scribbled beside it). Lots of photos of her grandad, who's always got a grin on his face ... the best one is of him crouched down on a beach with a stick in his hand – he's just used it to write *Sami Star* in the sand.

"Hey, Hannah ... what've you got there?" asks Vix.

My big sister is standing in the doorway of my bedroom. At first I think she's looking at the pile of *Diary Found* posters I made and printed off in the school library today. But, of course, Vix is more interested in the chunky blue book I've got open on my bed.

"It's a sort of diary," I tell her. "I found it in the park yesterday afternoon. Someone lost it."

I'm smiling as I speak, cos it's *so* nice that Vix is interested. It reminds me of how things used to be – my brilliant big sister who always had time for me, who was always fun. I've missed her a lot these last few weeks, when she's been so busy fighting with Mum and Dad all the time.

"Give us a look, then," says Vix. She comes into my room and plonks herself down beside me.

"It belongs to someone called Sami Star," I tell my sister as she turns the stiff pages. "I like the way there are more photos and drawings than words."

"An illustrated journal, you mean," murmurs Vix. "Wow, this is *so* cool, Hannah! Check out the trainers and lace-edged ankle socks. And the space buns with a headband ... that's a pretty cute look."

"Yeah, I was thinking I might try that," I say, twirling my hair with my fingers.

Normally, I just leave my long hair down. Robyn and Zadie both wear theirs up in a bun on the top of their heads. "Up or down," Robyn says. "Those are the *only* ways to do your hair." Ponytails, clips, hairbands, plaits are all a big fat no-no.

I've always gone along with that, but I'm not sure why.

"I love all these *Best things about today entries*," says Vix, reading one about Sami's dad making the best-ever masala chicken and another about how much fun it was playing two-pence slot machines in a seaside arcade with her grandad. "You know, if *I* had a diary like this, it would be all *WORST things about today*."

"Oh, Sami has some of those too!" I tell Vix as I flip the pages. "See? This one says,

Harry and Sofia teased me in class again and everyone laughed. Wish I had someone to stand up for me."

"Aw, poor Sami! I'd stand up for you!" says Vix, looking very sorry for this new person in our lives.

"And see here ..." I carry on flipping. "On this page, Sami says, *I miss Grandad so much. I miss HERE so much."*

"Do you think her grandad died, then?" asks Vix, looking at the photo beside this particular diary entry. It's of a caravan, which seems to be perched with others on a cliff. In the background is a great view of the sea.

"I suppose so," I agree. "What Sami's written is short, but it sounds sad ... more sad than if her grandad had just moved away or—"

"Hi girls! Can I come in?" says Mum, leaning on the door frame. She is smiling warmly at us, happy to see her daughters getting on so well. And that smile makes me smile too … could we be all right? Could we all just smile at each other and get back to normal? Vix isn't smiling, but she isn't scowling either, which is a start.

"We're looking at something I found," I answer Mum.

"That's nice," says Mum, but her eyes are fixed on Vix. She's not listening to anything I have to say. Seems like I'm still invisible. "So … I phoned the head of sixth form this afternoon."

"You did *what?*" snaps Vix, all her happiness bursting like popped bubblegum. "Mum, why on earth would you call Mr Lopez?"

"Well, I asked if you, me and Dad could all have a meeting with him about the problem," says Mum, and she folds her arms across her chest.

"What problem? I don't have a problem!" roars Vix as she jumps off the bed. "It's YOU that's got the problem. I'm sick of hearing about university. Don't you get it?"

Vix says this last part as she storms past Mum and vanishes into her own room with a *mammoth* slam of the door.

"Well, Victoria Mitchell, if you aren't going to university, don't think you're going to be lying about in your bed all day!" says Mum, following Vix and lecturing her from the other side of the door.

I hear a scream of anger from my sister's room.

OK, if Mum and Vix are busy growling at each other, I might as well go to the park again and get these posters up. It's been more than a day since poor Sami lost her diary, and she must be desperate to find it. Who knows – she could turn up to look for it. Maybe I'll meet her … maybe we'll chat and become friends!

I jump up off the bed – but feel a sharp spike stab my tummy. My stress pain has come back cos of all the shouting. As I try to slow-breathe it away, I catch sight of myself in the mirror. Long hair, pink hoodie, skinny jeans, white trainers. I look fine, but I look like everyone else. Will a girl as cool and kooky as Sami Star even be interested in me?

Maybe I'll be an invisible girl to her too …

Best thing about today...

smiling at this photo of
Grandad at the beach.

CHAPTER 4

THE LOST, THE FOUND AND THE CLUE

There ... the last poster is pinned to the fence near the tennis courts.

I've dotted lots of posters all around the park. The first one I stuck up was on the tree right next to the bench where me, Robyn and Zadie came across Sami's lost diary.

I thought I might see Sami there, but no luck. And I've been looking round the park for the last twenty minutes in the hope that I'll spot her, but I haven't seen anyone who might be Sami Star.

I grin now, thinking how funny it is to be searching for a girl whose face you've never even seen. Instead, I've been keeping an eye out for some of the shoes, socks and patterned-tights combinations I've seen in the Polaroid photos. Or dark brown hair in some interesting style, with mad hairclips or zany headbands.

But the park has just been full of tiny kids and chatting mums, plus a few teenagers who look like me.

Actually, right this minute I do *not* look like me!

Before I left to come here, I spun my hair up into two little space buns. I also scrabbled at the back of my sock drawer and found a pair of purple and white polka-dot socks that I used to love but haven't worn for ages. I've turned up my jeans so you can see them.

OK, so I might not be a full-on Sami Star, but I'm a more interesting version of Hannah Mitchell!

I stop grinning when I notice I'm being stared at. Hard.

"Hi!" I say, and give a shy wave to Robyn and Zadie, who are walking towards me. They're looking at me as if I've grown a unicorn horn.

"Hi ..." they mutter back together. Their eyes roam up and down me. I feel the opposite of invisible now – my friends can *definitely* see me. And it's pretty obvious they don't like what they see.

"What are you doing, Hannah?" asks Zadie.

I'm not sure if she's talking about the poster they must have seen me putting up or my space buns and spotty socks.

"I made these *Found* posters, in case Sami's looking for her diary," I tell them, pointing at the fence. I suddenly see the glitter on my finger. I was copying a look I saw in one of Sami's headshots. As usual, her face wasn't in the picture, but I just made out a sparkle of glitter under the corner of her eyebrow.

Robyn and Zadie both blink at me slowly with their perfectly black-winged eyes.

"Don't know why you're bothering," says Robyn.

Both my friends thought I was mad when I told them at school today that I'd rescued the diary. Zadie was so shocked when I told her about how I'd grubbed about in the bin to get the diary back that she nearly choked on her tuna pasta at lunch.

"Well, if I lost something, I'd be really happy if someone found it and tried to give it back to me," I tell them.

"Yeah, but you wouldn't be drifting around the park with something as rubbish as that so-called diary, Hannah," says Zadie.

When Zadie talks about drifting around the park, I suddenly realise I've got something to ask my two best friends.

"What are *you* doing here anyway?" I ask. They didn't say anything about coming here after school today.

"Oh, uh ... Zadie was talking to Dan and Krish in Science last lesson," says Robyn, looking embarrassed. "They said they might hang out here at the park, so ..."

So, it looks like Sami isn't the only one to have lost something. I think I might be losing my best friends. They've been getting less kind, less fun for a while now. And today they're more interested in two random boys than me.

"Isn't that Dan and Krish over there?" I say, pointing to the yelling idiots trying to run up the slide in the kids' playground.

"Oh, yeah!" says Zadie, moving off without even looking at me.

"Um ... do you want to come?" Robyn asks. She doesn't look keen. I suppose me and my space buns and glitter eye-shadow might embarrass her and Zadie in front of the boys.

"No – I have to get back home," I say, and give Robyn a wave as I walk away.

That's a lie, of course. I don't *have* to get home. *The way things are, no one will notice if I'm there or not*, I think sadly.

Then all of a sudden I have the strangest tickly feeling in my chest – I really, truly *wish* I could talk to Sami Star!

Flicking through her diary, it's like I found a new friend. But how can I say that about someone I don't really know? Someone who doesn't even know I exist?

Maybe that'll change if she sees the poster and calls my number. And wait – if she doesn't see it, perhaps there's another way I can meet Sami Star.

I hurry over to a nearby bench, pull her diary out of my bag and flick to the page with the clue I've just remembered ...

Best thing about today ...

remembering the fun I had with
Grandad at the fair last year.

It's coming to the seafront again
this Saturday, and I'm going to go –
I don't care what anyone says.

CHAPTER 5
THE SEASIDE SEARCH

Yesterday afternoon, I had a crazy idea of how I might hook up with Sami Star. This afternoon, I'm sitting next to my sister and we're suspended high, high, high in the sky ...

What happened in between then and now?

Well, it started with the clue in Sami's diary. It was the entry from last Monday, to be exact. There was a sort-of-selfie on it – Sami's face was hidden by a big sugary fluff of candy-floss and there was a huge Ferris wheel in the background.

Beside the photo, Sami had written, *Best thing about today: remembering the fun I had with Grandad at the fair last year. It's coming to the seafront again this Saturday, and I'm going to go – I don't care what anyone says.*

I stared at the photo.

A fair, by the sea, that was on this Saturday – *there* was my clue.

Back home, I googled all the seaside towns near us and – *blam!* – I found what I was looking for! A fair was happening in Stanport this weekend.

So I'd worked out where Sami might be this Saturday.

Next, I had to figure out how to get there and who'd take me. Someone who wouldn't think I was acting crazy ...

Which brings me back to *this* afternoon.

"You're crazy, Hannah, and I'm crazy for coming with you," says Vix now.

It's 3 p.m. and we're at the top of the Ferris wheel, with the most amazing view. The fair and higgledy-piggledy town of Stanport is below us, and the dancing waves of the sea stretch to the horizon.

Not that Vix can see any of it. Her hands are over her eyes.

"You mean you're really *kind* for taking me here," I correct her as I stare down at the crowds below because maybe I'll spot a hairstyle I'll recognise.

We took the bus here and we've walked around the fair for the last two hours, but we haven't seen anyone who might be Sami Star.

"I could've been chilling in my room this afternoon instead of getting vertigo on this stupid ride," Vix grumbles.

"You were glad to get away," I remind her. "You said another day at home with Mum and Dad nagging you would drive you up the wall."

"Yeah, I suppose I *did* say that," Vix says as she bravely peeks between her fingers. "But can I ask you something, Hannah? Why didn't you just try and find this mystery girl in a more normal way? I mean, Sami Star is a pretty weird name and *must* be easy to search ... isn't she on Instagram or something?"

"I tried that the day I found the diary," I tell my sister. "But I couldn't find her anywhere ..."

Hopefully I'll be lucky and find Sami Star here today in Stanford. I lean forward on the metal bar that holds us in, still searching, still scanning.

"Ouch!" I squeak. A dart of pain pinches me in the stomach.

"You OK?" asks Vix, and drops her hands away from her face. Worry about me wins over her fear of heights – which is nice to know.

"Yeah, sure. Mum would just say I've eaten too much rubbish," I tell Vix as I rub the pain away with my hand.

"Hmm ... hotdogs and candy-floss aren't exactly a healthy lunch, I suppose," says Vix. "Maybe Mum's right – for once."

I look over at Vix. After talking about Mum, she's gone all quiet.

"Can I ask *you* a question?" I say to my sister.

It's something I've wanted to ask her for a while, but I've been worried that she'll yell at me like she yells at our parents.

"Sure – what is it?" says Vix. She's gripping the metal bar so tight her knuckles are white.

"When Mum and Dad ask you what you're going to do if you don't go to university, instead of getting angry why don't you just tell them?" I ask.

Vix is silent for a few seconds.

"It's cos I don't know myself, Hannah," she says at last. "I want to have time to think it over, but Mum and Dad won't let me. I just wish—"

Pling!!

There's an alert on Vix's phone. She twists it out of her pocket and reads what's on the screen – then turns to me and frowns.

"What is it?" I ask, feeling a flutter of worry in my tummy as well as rumbles of pain.

"It's a friend from sixth form," Vix answers. "She's just shared something on our Snapchat group. Hannah, you've got to look at this ..."

The wind up here whips my hair in front of my face, but as I tuck it behind my ears I see the message Vix is holding up for me to read:

MISSING TWELVE-YEAR-OLD –
PLEASE HELP!

Our daughter Sami has been missing since this morning. She never goes out without telling us where she's going. She has been very sad after her grandad's death and has been bullied at school. Something very special has been stolen from her too. But she has Asperger's and is quite vulnerable. Please share – we need our sweet girl home!

And there is a photo.

Sami.

My Sami.

A serious-looking girl with a kooky sense of style. Her big brown eyes have the longest lashes. She seems to stare out of the photo straight at me.

"Hello, Sami Star," I mutter to my never-met friend. "Where are you?"

"Hey, look over there!" Vix cries.

She's pointing to a cliff at the far end of the beach.

A cliff with caravans teetering on the edge.

The Ferris wheel can't get down to the ground fast enough ...

Best thing about today...

thinking about Grandad's caravan.

CHAPTER 6
SUNFLOWERS AND RED BLOOMS

"Let's see the photo again," says Vix as we hurry closer to the caravans that line the cliff edge.

"Here," I say as I hold up Sami's diary. It's open at a page she wrote a few weeks ago, with a photo of her grandad's caravan. I'm panting, as out of breath as my sister. There's now a low, grumbling pain in my tummy that's making it hard for me to breathe, but I'm more worried about finding Sami Star.

"OK, so her grandad's caravan is the same as all the others except it's got all these plants around it," Vix goes on as she stabs her finger at the photo and the cheerful sunflowers it shows.

"There!" I burst out. I point to a caravan with plastic plant pots dotted all around. Sad stumps of wilted brown stalks flop in them. The dead flowers give me hope – no one has bothered to plant fresh ones, so that must mean there isn't a new owner yet. It *might* mean Sami is here, inside.

I slap the diary shut, and me and Vix speed up. My heart is racing as much as my tummy is aching. If I knock at the caravan door, will *she* open it?

"Hannah, look!" Vix says, and grabs at my arm.

My legs suddenly turn to jelly. Just beyond the caravan with the plant pots, and all the

other matching caravans, is a low stone wall.
A wall that must run the whole way along the
cliff edge.

And standing by the wall, leaning over it, is a girl. She's wearing denim shorts and stripy tights with purple Converse baseball boots. A hand-knitted sky-blue jumper. Hair in plaits, fixed with flowery bobbles. A small dog on a lead waits at her feet.

I run ahead of Vix.

"Sami?" I call out as softly as I can. I don't want to scare her – she's so close to the edge it looks dangerous.

The pug sees me and barks. The girl turns just as I get to her side. Her deep brown eyes are pooled with tears. They stare into mine, and I know she's asking herself who I am and how I know her name.

I notice that she has a bunch of sunflowers in one hand.

"I'm Hannah," I begin.

But I don't get any further. A red raw pain suddenly blooms in my tummy, and I can't move with the shock of it.

But then I *am* moving – a gust of wind slaps me in the back so hard that I tilt and stumble sideways.

The pain makes my reactions slow. My hands don't grab at the wall in time to get my balance.

I gasp as I find myself staring down at thundering crests of waves, where a single sunflower bobs on the surface before being swallowed into the depths.

Uh, oh, I think, *I'm next ...*

CHAPTER 7
WHO RESCUED WHO?

"Hi, Hannah!" says Robyn as she and Zadie amble up to the school gate.

I see Zadie staring at my hair. I've got it in plaits today, with shiny red-cherry bobbles. I love them. I don't care if no one else does.

"Hi," I say, and wave at my old friends.

We're still friends, though these days more distant, *hi-how-are-you-doing* kind of friends.

"Sami's just coming – I saw her mum dropping her off," says Zadie.

I'm glad Robyn and Zadie are nice to Sami. Like just about everyone in town, they know what happened a few weeks ago. They know Sami went missing, that me and Vix found her, that my appendix burst and I fainted with the pain and nearly fell from the cliff.

They know I went from *rescuing Sami Star* to *Sami Star rescuing me.* If she hadn't grabbed me, I'd have been the one missing ... missing at sea.

But just cos Robyn and Zadie are nice to Sami, it doesn't mean they totally get her. They think her Asperger's makes her a *lot* more different than she actually is.

I mean, yes, Sami gets a bit freaked out by too much noise and the crush of crowds at class changeover. Yes, she doesn't smile much, even when she's really, really happy. Yes, there's a bunch of other small things that make Sami ... well, Sami. And I find them all interesting.

In the last few weeks, our family and Sami's have become good friends. Sami and her parents came to visit me in the hospital to say thank you for finding her. Mum and Dad invited them all round for tea once I was back home, to say thank you for saving me.

By the way, Sami and my sister sort of saved each other too. Since we got to know Sami, Vix has been reading everything she can about Asperger's and autism. And after her A levels, next term Vix is going to volunteer at a primary school for children with autism. If things work out there, she might stay on as a teaching assistant. Or maybe in another year or two she could go to university and train to be a teacher who specialises in autism. (She hasn't told Mum and Dad that yet, in case they never shut up about it!)

And it was Vix who talked to Sami's parents about switching her from her old school to ours. Sami's not great with change, but this is

one that *really* worked. Being away from the
bullies who teased her and stole and dumped
her diary has totally been the best thing for
her.

"Come on, Sami Shah! The bell's about to
go!" the teacher at the gate calls out cheerfully.

And here comes my best friend, running
along the pavement, her hair flying out behind
her, the bow on her patterned headband
fluttering like a butterfly.

"Yeah, come on, Sami Star!" I call out, using
the nickname her grandad gave her.

"Wait for me, Hannah!" shouts Sami.

"Always," I say back with a smile.

Sami's eyes glow as she draws close and
high-fives the hand I'm holding up to her.

Cos now we're friends, Sami Star knows the future is shiny bright for *both* of us ...

Thursday 19th

Best thing about today...

just hanging out with my
<u>best</u> <u>friend</u>, =Hannah!=

Our books are tested
for children and young people by
children and young people.

Thanks to everyone who consulted on
a manuscript for their time and effort in
helping us to make our books better
for our readers.